I like green

by Wendy Body

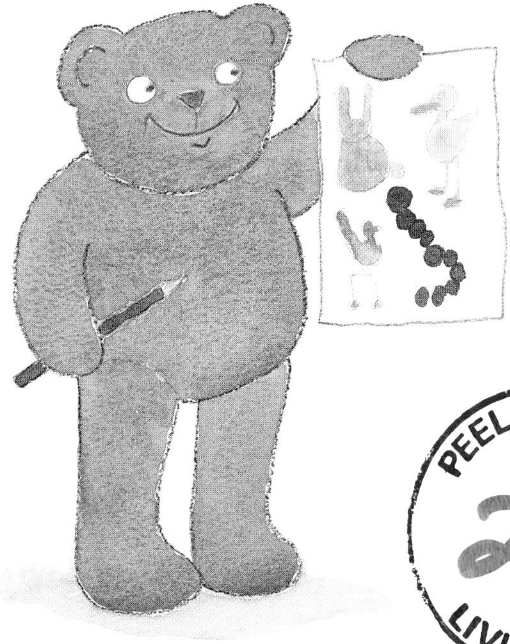

PEEL PRIMARY
21
LIVINGSTON

Illustrated by Adrienne Geoghegan

W0006426

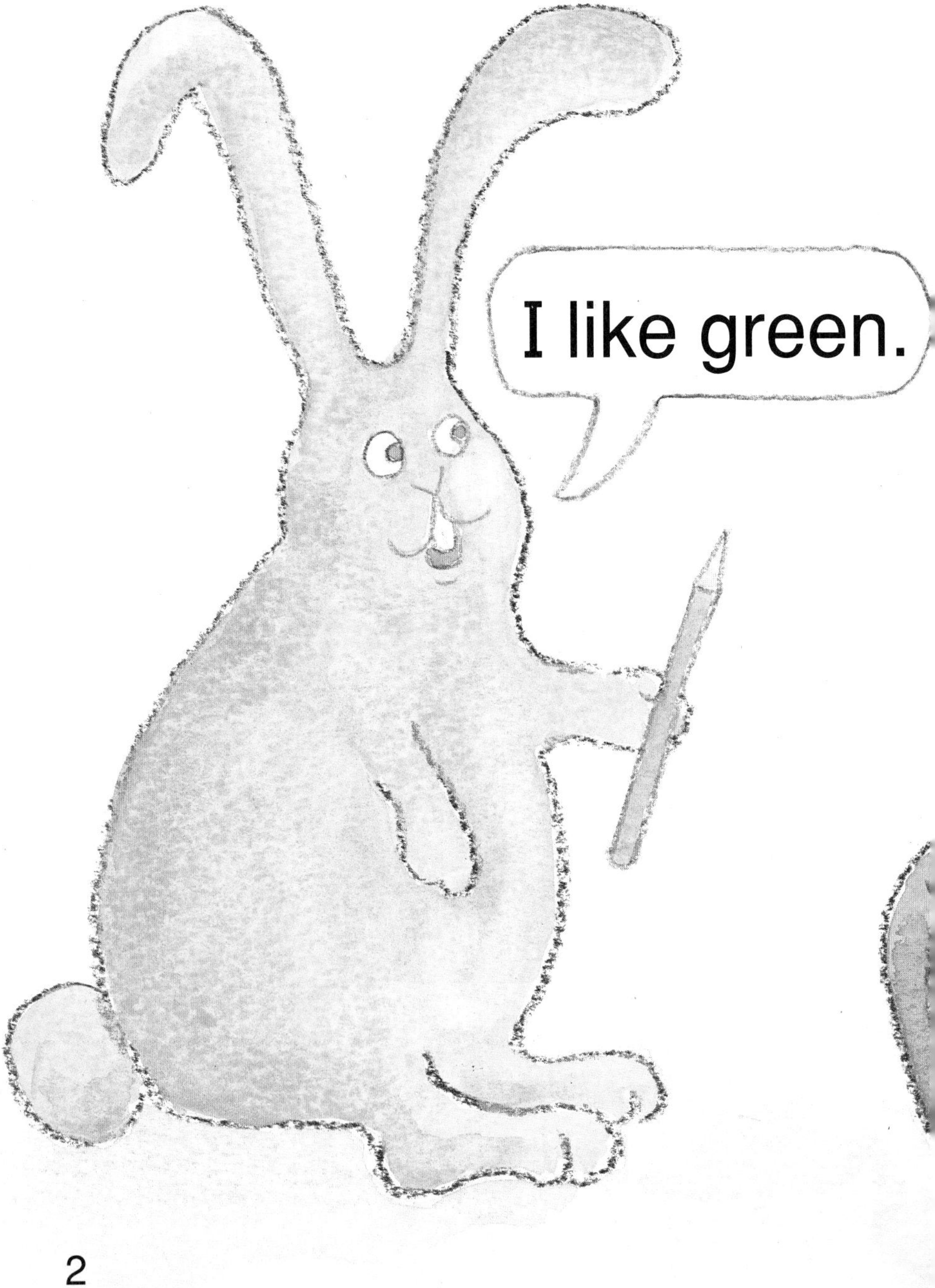
I like green.

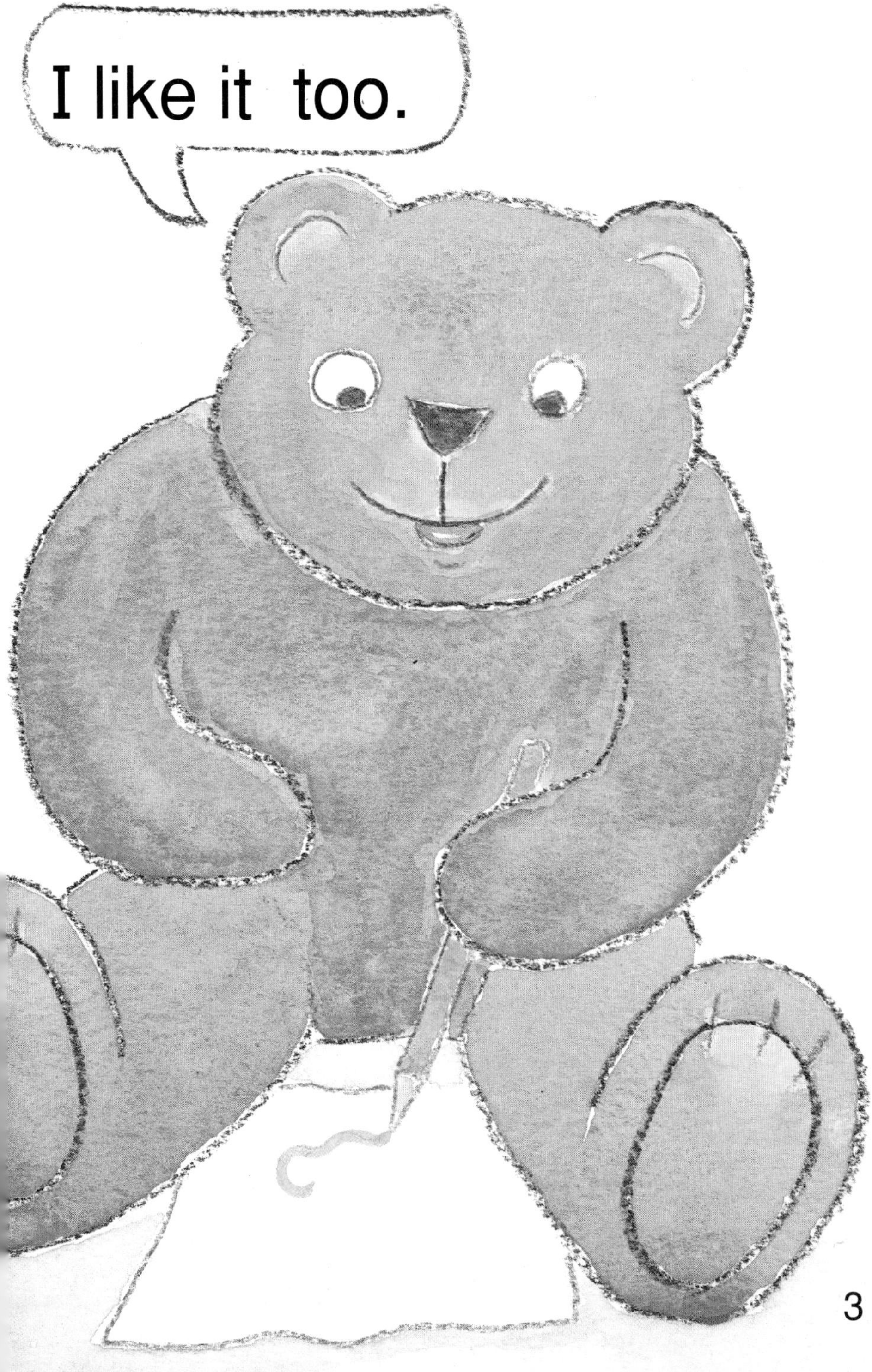
I like it too.

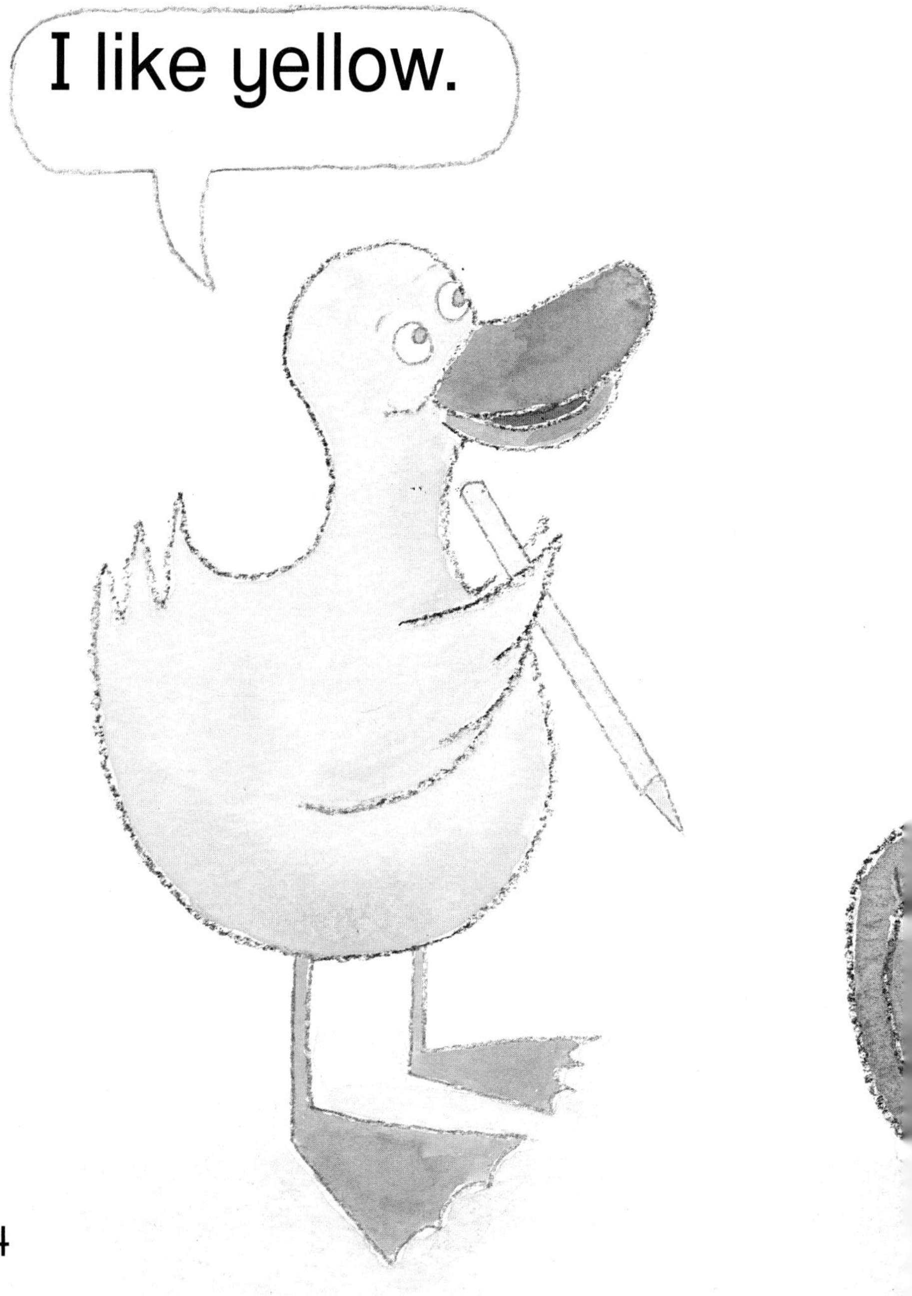
I like yellow.

I like it too.

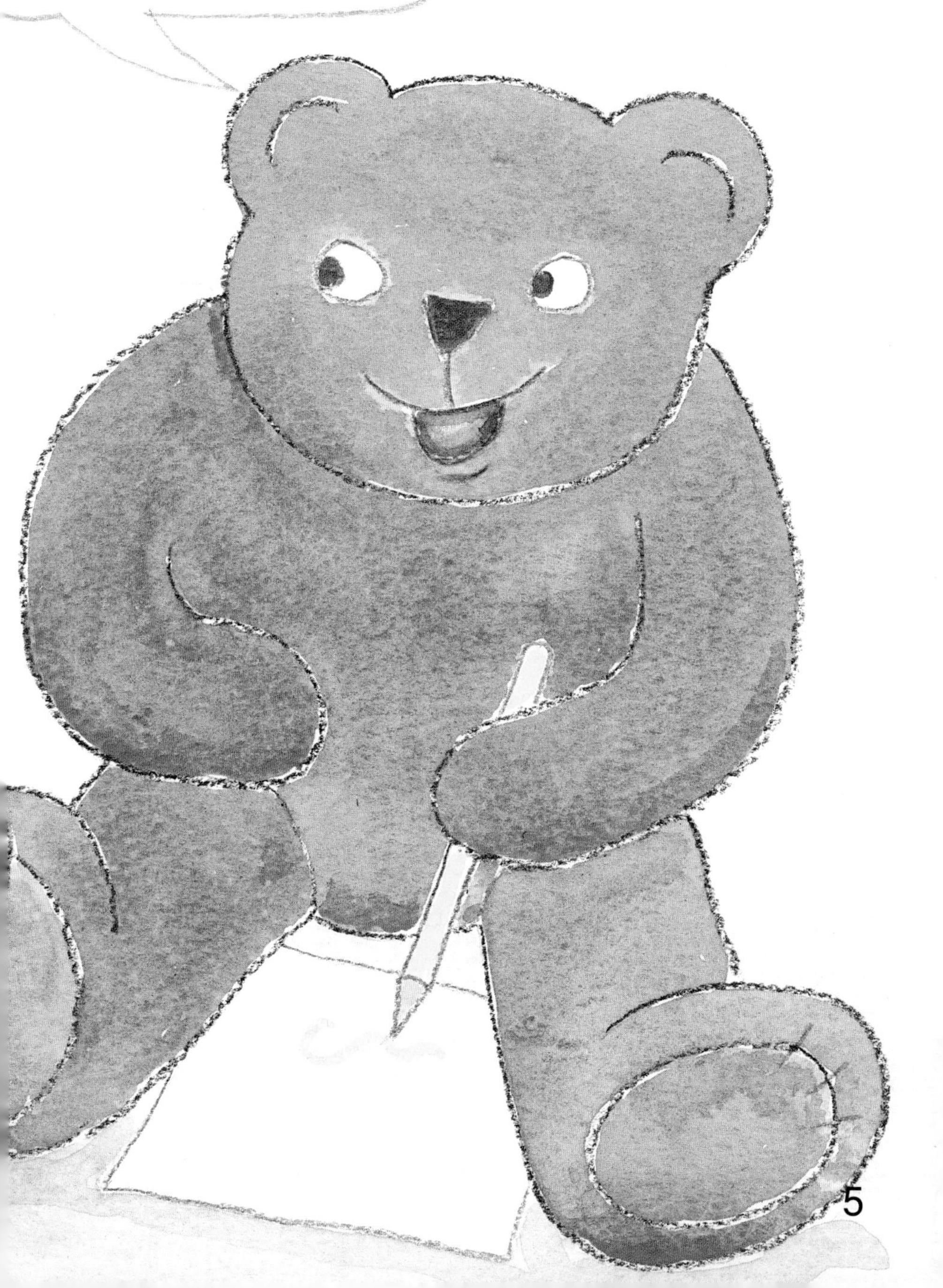

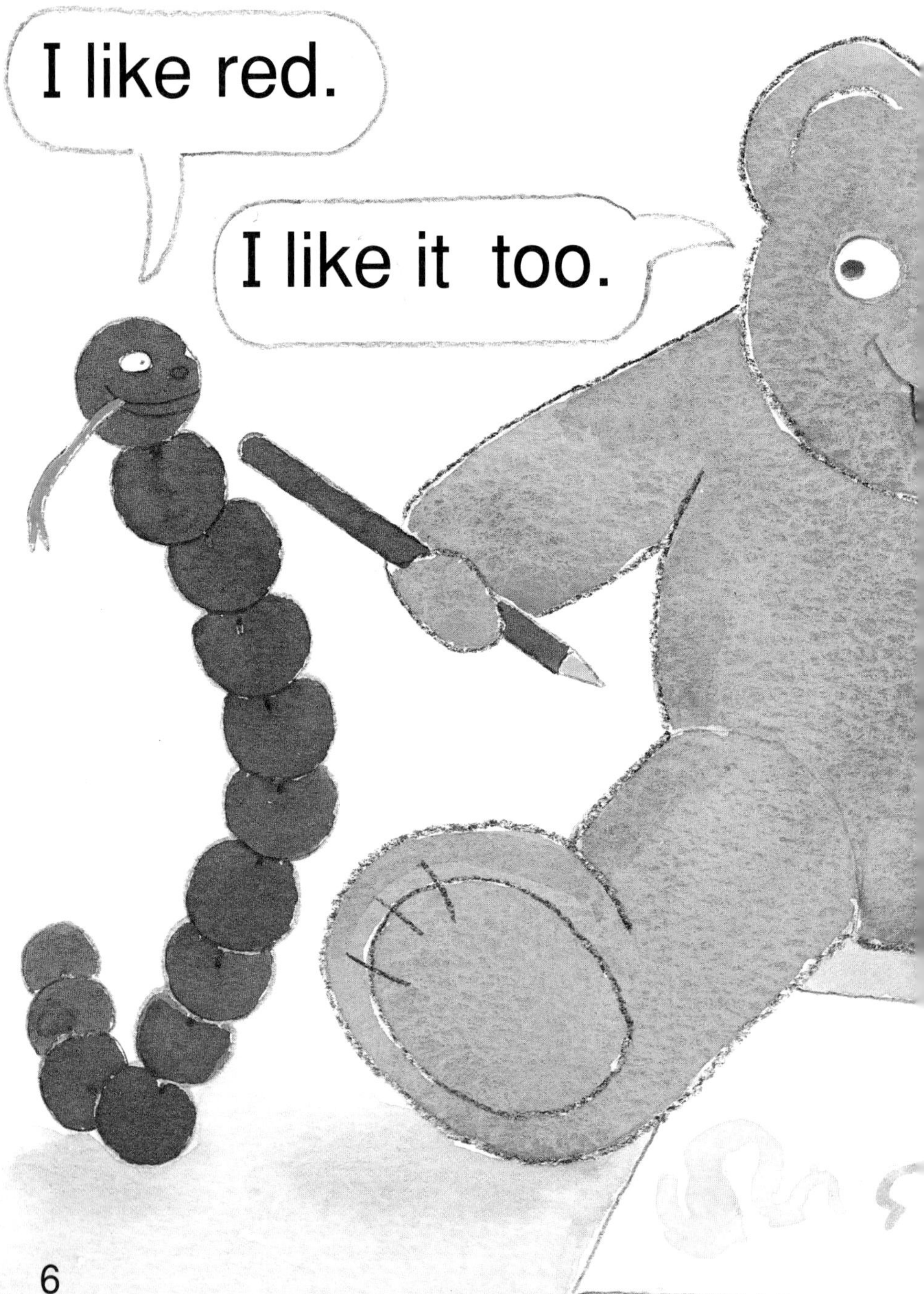
I like red.
I like it too.

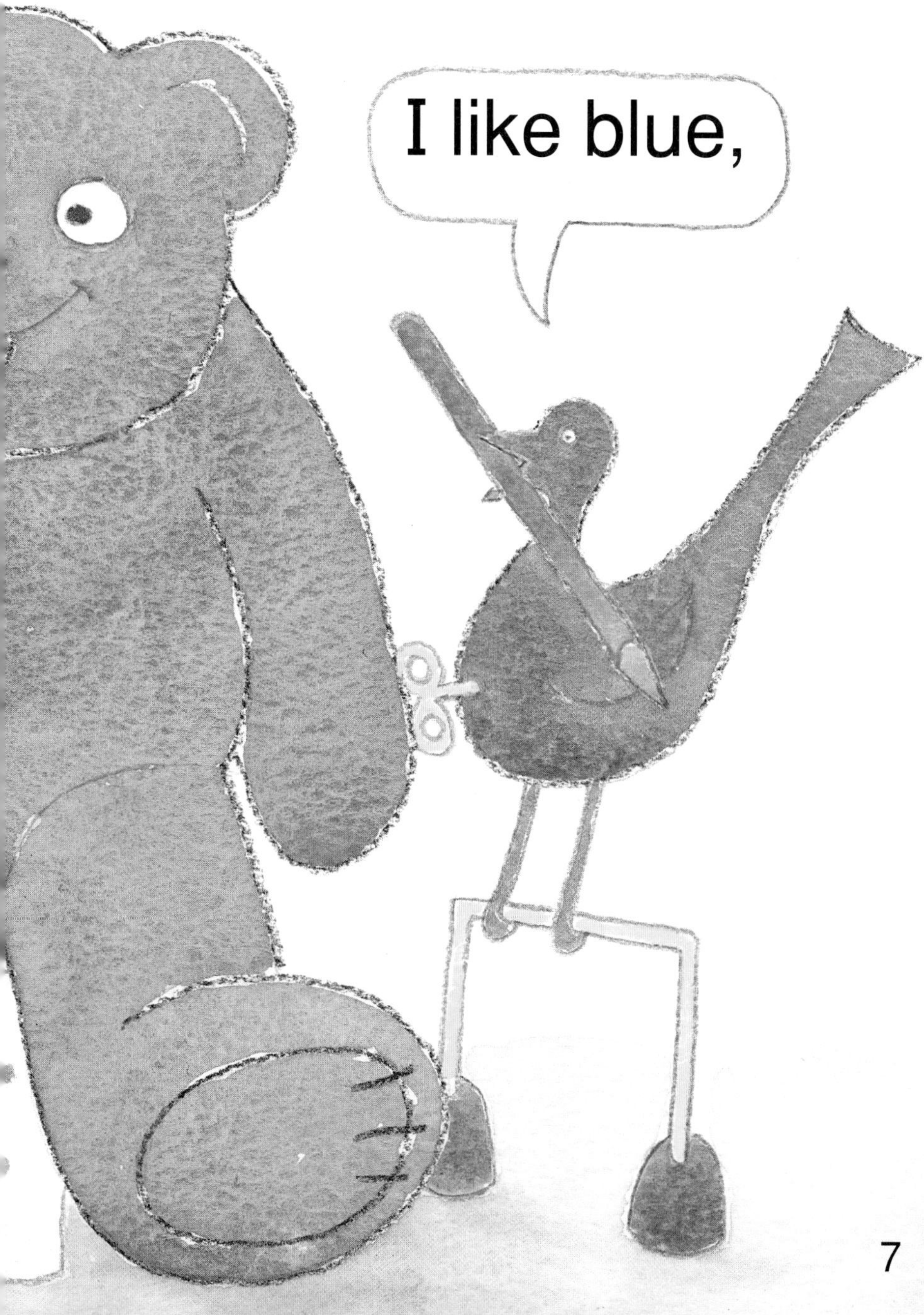
I like blue,

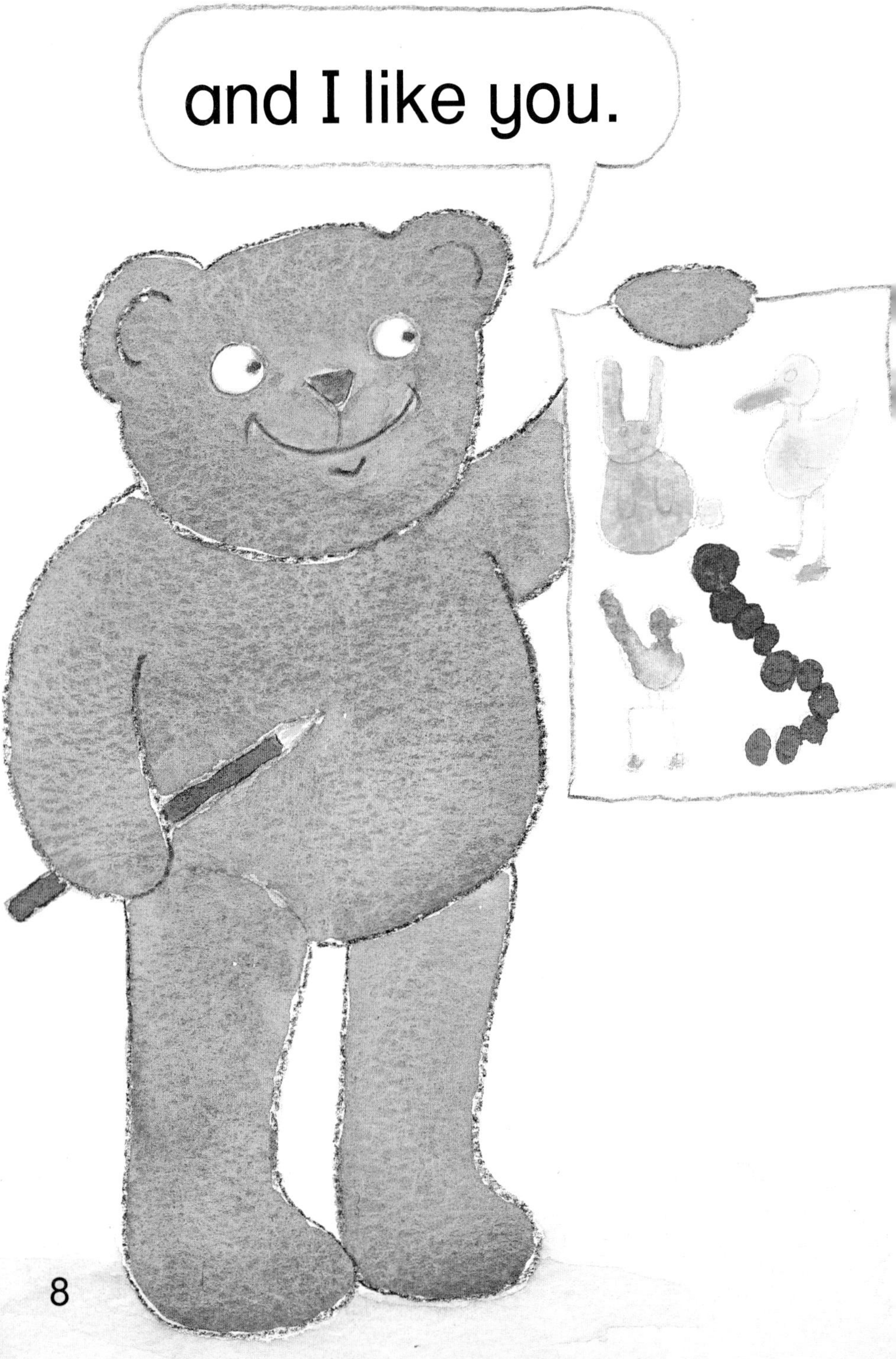
and I like you.